Race Ahead with Reading

# The Pirate Pie Ship

by Adam and Charlotte Guillain

Illustrated by Rupert Van Wyk

W
FRANKLIN WATTS
LONDON • SYDNEY

# Chapter 1

The Planktown Pirates were tired. They were tired of scaring sailors. They were tired of chasing other ships. They were tired of digging for treasure.

And most of all, they were tired of fighting their pirate rivals, the Gruesome Crew.

"I feel like trying something new," sighed Captain Cuttlefish.

"But what?" asked Manta Ray Jack, the ship's First Mate.

"Being pirates is all we know," moaned Connor the Cabin Boy.

Cook Cockles watched the crew slump in despair. He decided to cook the Captain's favourite, Octopus and Seaweed pie, for lunch.

"This pie will help you think of ideas," said Cook Cockles. He served up a steaming slice of pie for the Captain.

Captain Cuttlefish ate a mouthful of pie. Then he ate another. A twinkle came into his eye as he looked around at the crew gobbling down their lunch.

"That's it!" he cried. The crew looked up,
but they didn't stop eating.

"Your delicious pies are the
finest on the seven seas,"
the captain told Cook Cockles.
"We can sell them in the port
and make our fortune!"

The crew cheered and raised their
mugs of lemonade.

"Here's to the Planktown Pirates' Pie Ship!"
bellowed Captain Cuttlefish.

"Now, let's get making pies!"

# Chapter 2

For the rest of the day, the pirates worked hard catching fish. In the galley, Cook Cockles turned the crew into trainee chefs.

They chopped and scraped ...

and stirred ...

and baked.

Soon the first batch of pies was ready.

"Set sail for the port!" shouted the Captain.

"Full speed ahead!"

The crew leapt into action.

Connor the Cabin Boy had painted

*The Pirate Pie Ship* in big letters on the

largest sail. The skull and crossbones had

been taken down and a new flag was flying.

As the ship sailed into the port, a large group of hungry sailors was waiting. The smell of delicious pies wafted over the port and the sailors raced across and jostled into a line.

"Today's specials are Anchovy and
Algae pie, and Sardine and Seagrass pie,"
shouted Manta Ray Jack.
"Roll up! Roll up! Three gold coins
for a pie!"

Soon the pirates had sold every single pie and the sailors were begging them to come back the next day. Captain Cuttlefish sat on the deck and counted coins.

"This beats digging for treasure! We'll soon be rich!" the crew cheered.

None of the pirates noticed the Gruesome

Crew's ship sailing silently into the port.

And nobody noticed they were being

watched through a telescope.

# Chapter 3

The next morning the happy pirates

set to work making more pies.

At midday they set sail for the port again.

They could see another line of starving

sailors waiting for them.

But as they got closer to the port,

another ship appeared from behind the cliff

and sailed speedily up to the hungry sailors.

"My telescope! Now!" shouted

Captain Cuttlefish. He held it to

his eye and stared at the other ship.

"Curses and barnacles!" he roared.

"It's the Gruesome Crew! Their ship

has always been faster than ours."

Captain Cuttlefish looked more closely. He

could see *The Gruesome Fish and Chip Ship*

painted on the side of the enemy ship.

The Gruesome Crew were laughing as they served up huge plates of fish and chips to the line of eager customers. Their leader, Captain Sharkfin, was counting piles and piles of gold and silver coins.

"Sail faster!" shouted
Captain Cuttlefish.

But by the time the Planktown Pirates
reached the port, all the sailors had
licked their plates and gone. There
wasn't a single customer left.

"This means war!" Captain Cuttlefish shouted at the Gruesome Crew, as their ship drew alongside their jeering enemies. "You'll never win!" sneered Captain Sharkfin, with an evil laugh.

## Chapter 4

The next morning the pirates set to work catching fish and making pies again. Connor the Cabin Boy jumped in a rowing boat and set off for the port.

When he arrived, he put up a sign saying
'Mullet and Kelp Pie' and stood holding
a large, empty basket. The hungry sailors
saw Connor's sign but were disappointed
that he had no pies to sell.

"Your pies are the most delicious food

around," said one sailor.

"And the Gruesome Crew aren't very

friendly. But we're all so hungry

by lunchtime we'll always eat

fish and chips if they get here first."

And sure enough, at midday the
Gruesome Crew's ship sailed swiftly
into the port. The smell of chips
blew in on the wind and the sailors
started to line up.

# Chapter 5

"Wait!" shouted Connor, waving a flag.

# BOOM!

The sailors all turned to see what

the noise was.

# BOOM!

Out at sea, the Plankton Pirates' ship was firing its cannons right at the port!

# BOOM!

# BOOM!

The Gruesome Fish and chip Ship

Connor held up his basket and started to catch the piping hot pies that were being fired from the ship. They smelled delicious!

The sailors gasped and turned back to Connor, who happily handed out pies and took gold coins.

The Gruesome Crew could only watch

as all the sailors munched on the hot pies.

Then they looked up at their ship's masts.

The pies had shot straight through

the sails and they were in tatters!

The Gruesome Crew wouldn't be sailing

anywhere for a while.

As the sailors munched the last
of their pies, the Planktown Pirates
sailed cheering into the port.

Captain Cuttlefish was holding

up another huge pie.

"Chocolate and cherry pie for everyone!"

he shouted.

And all the sailors

jumped aboard

for pudding.

First published in 2012 by
Franklin Watts
338 Euston Road
London
NW1 3BH

Franklin Watts Australia
Level 17/207 Kent Street
Sydney
NSW 2000

Text © Adam and Charlotte Guillain 2012
Illustration © Rupert Van Wyk 2012

The rights of Adam and Charlotte Guillain
to be identified as the author and Rupert Van
Wyk as the illustrator of this Work have been
asserted in accordance with the Copyright,
Designs and Patents Act, 1988.

**Series Editor:** Melanie Palmer
**Series Advisor:** Catherine Glavina
**Series Designer:** Peter Scoulding

All rights reserved. No part of this
publication may be reproduced, stored
in a retrieval system, or transmitted in
any form or by any means, electronic,
mechanical, photocopy, recording or
otherwise, without the prior written
permission of the copyright owner.

A CIP catalogue record for this book is
available from the British Library.

ISBN 978 1 4451 0773 8 (hbk)
ISBN 978 1 4451 0779 0 (pbk)

Printed in China

Franklin Watts is a division of Hachette
Children's Books, an Hachette UK company.
www.hachette.co.uk